MW00903786

MEET ALL THESE FRIENDS IN BUZZ BOOKS:

Thomas the Tank Engine
Fireman Sam
The Animals of Farthing Wood
Skeleton Warriors
Puppy In My Pocket
Kitty In My Pocket
Pony In My Pocket

First published in Great Britain in 1996 by Buzz Books
an imprint of Reed Children's Books
Michelin House, 81 Fulham Road, London SW3 6RB
and Auckland, Melbourne, Singapore and Toronto.

Based on a Martin Gates Production
Copyright ©1996 BMG Entertainment
Licensed by Just Licensing Ltd
Text copyright © 1996 Reed International Books Limited
Illustrations by Arkadia copyright © 1996 Reed International Books Limited

ISBN 1 85591 553 7

Printed in Italy

Wild Wood Adventure

Story by Katie Vandyck
from the animated series

One autumn afternoon, Mole and Rat were sitting together in Rat's parlour. A small fire burned in the grate and they were both feeling very cosy.

"Rat?" asked Mole. "When do you suppose I shall be able to meet Badger?"

"Oh, Badger will turn up some day or other," Rat answered vaguely.

Mole was disappointed. He tried again.

"Couldn't we ask him for dinner or something?"

Rat explained
that Badger hated
being invited to things.
He didn't like people to
arrive unannounced either.

"Besides," he added, "he lives in the
Wild Wood."

"You told me the Wild Wood was all
right," persisted Mole.

Rat looked worried.

"Oh, I know, I know, so it is. He'll
be coming along some day, if you'll
wait quietly."

Mole sighed and looked out of the window.

The days became shorter and the wind sharper as autumn turned into winter. One afternoon, while Rat sat dozing in front of the fire, Mole decided to go and find Mr Badger for himself.

"Ratty," he addressed the sleeping form.

Rat replied with a gentle snore.

"Ratty, I can't sit in this chair a moment longer. I shall go and explore the Wild Wood and if you won't come with me I shall go on my own."

There was no reply. Mole put on his coat, hat and galoshes and tiptoed to the door. He closed it quietly behind him and stepped out into the wintery landscape.

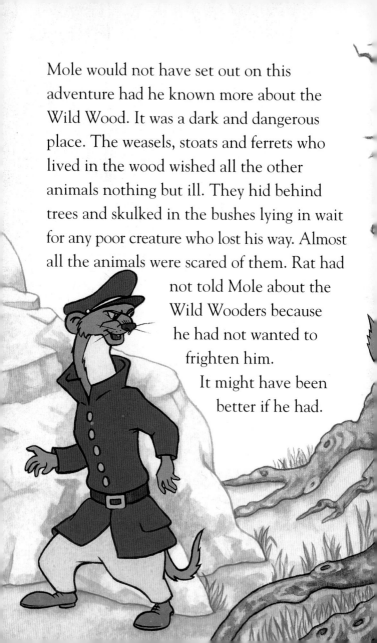

Mole would not have set out on this
adventure had he known more about the
Wild Wood. It was a dark and dangerous
place. The weasels, stoats and ferrets who
lived in the wood wished all the other
animals nothing but ill. They hid behind
trees and skulked in the bushes lying in wait
for any poor creature who lost his way. Almost
all the animals were scared of them. Rat had
not told Mole about the
Wild Wooders because
he had not wanted to
frighten him.
It might have been
better if he had.

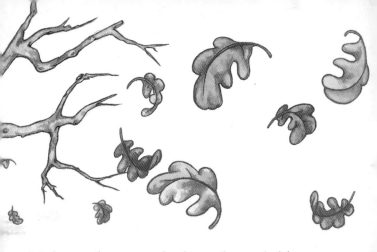

Mole strode across the bare, frosty fields, humming to himself as he went. He reached the Wild Wood and at first was able to follow a path. The further he walked into the wood, however, the darker it became. The shadows became denser and Mole began to feel that he was being watched.

Each time he heard a rustle, he spun round only to find nothing there. A low whistling started up in the undergrowth. It seemed to come from all around him. He hurried along, trying to escape the noise but, in his panic, he stumbled off the path and plunged into the thick wood.

It wasn't long before Mole realised he
was lost.

"Oh dear, oh dear. I wish I'd brought Rat's
big stick," he moaned.

By now he was surrounded by the sound
of pattering footsteps. A rabbit dashed out
of the undergrowth, nearly knocking
him down.

"Get out of here, you fool, get out!" hissed the rabbit before he disappeared.

Mole started to run. Weasel-like figures darted out at him from the dark. Hungry weasel eyes gleamed wickedly at him from the bushes. He ran and ran. He stumbled blindly into tree trunks and tripped over branches. Suddenly he spotted a black hole at the foot of a tree and dived in.

"Oh, oh, help, help," he whispered.

Back in his parlour Rat awoke with a start. Seeing that Mole's coat was missing, he realised with horror where he had gone. He grabbed hold of his walking stick, and, after a moment's thought, seized a couple of pistols. He hastened out after Mole. Rat strode bravely through the darkening wood calling out for his friend. The rustling noises and pattering footsteps died away as the shadowy weasels realised who the brave creature was.

"Look out," they whispered. "It's Rat. He's armed. Be careful."

At last Rat came upon the shivering Mole and, after a joyful meeting, persuaded the frightened animal that they should start for home as soon as possible. He let Mole rest for a while but when they came out of the hole they discovered that the ground was covered with snow.

"Well, well, it can't be helped," said Rat. They tried to find their way out but the snow had made the wood unrecognisable and soon they were lost.

"Oh, Ratty, whatever shall we do?" asked Mole tearfully.

"We might try and find some sort of shelter," said Rat, looking about him.

As he spoke Mole tripped and fell headlong into the snow.

"Aw!" he cried.

He winced as he rubbed his injured leg.
Rat examined the wound and looked
puzzled.

"It looks as if it was made by the sharp
edge of something metal."

Suddenly he leapt to his feet and capered
about for joy.

"Hooray-oo-ray-ooray-oo-ray," he sang.
Mole had tripped over a door scraper and, as
Rat explained, where there was a door
scraper, there must be a door.

Rat began to dig furiously and called to Mole to join in. Finally their labours were rewarded. In the side of what had seemed to be a snow bank they discovered a solid-looking little door with a small brass plate. Neatly engraved in square capital letters were the words "Mr Badger".

Mole tumbled backwards into the snow with delight.

"Rat, you're a wonder!" he cried.

Rat started hammering loudly on the door with his stick and after an interval the door opened and a snout and a pair of blinking eyes appeared.

It was Mr Badger.

MR
BADGER

Mr Badger stood in the doorway holding a candle. He was dressed for bed and looked furious. "Now, the next time this happens, I shall be exceedingly angry," he growled.

Rat cried out, "Oh, Badger, let us in, please. It's me, Rat. We've lost our way in the snow."

When Mr Badger realised who it was he was quick to welcome them in. The two animals tumbled over each other in their eagerness to get inside. Badger led Rat and Mole along endless gloomy tunnels until they came to his kitchen. It was warm and inviting and before long the tired wanderers were settled in front of a huge fire feeling most content.

Later that evening as they sat down to eat,
Badger asked the animals:

"Tell us the news from your part of the
world. How's old Toad going on?"

"From bad to worse," replied Rat, and
told Badger about Toad's latest motor-car
smash-up.

"This is his seventh; his coach house is
piled up to the roof with fragments of
motor-cars."

Mole joined in, "He's been in hospital three times, and as for the fines he's had to pay . . . " He shook his head sadly.

The animals agreed that Toad needed sorting out.

"But now it's time for bed," Badger said firmly.

After a good sleep, the two animals came down very late for breakfast. The door bell rang and seconds later Otter bounced into the room and flung his arms round Rat.

"Ratty!" he cried.

"Get off!" spluttered Rat, his mouth full of toast.

Otter was relieved to find that both Mole and Rat were safe. All their river bank friends had been most anxious at their disappearance. Otter had guessed that they might find their way to Badger's house and had gone straight there.

"You came through the Wild Wood?" asked Mole, impressed.

"And the snow," boasted Otter. Mole looked at him in awe.

Badger came into the kitchen, yawning and rubbing his eyes. He greeted Otter warmly and the four animals sat down to a hearty meal. At last Rat patted his stomach and sighed.

"This is all very enjoyable, but Mole and I must get off while it's daylight. We don't want another night in the Wild Wood," he said.

Otter took the lead and brought them safely through the Wild Wood and out into the sunlight. They made their way across the fields until at last they could see the river gleaming in the distance.

"Home!" said Rat, thankfully.

"Home!" echoed Mole as he trotted after him towards the bright welcoming landscape ahead of them.